To every town's witches, hermits, and Boo Radleys;
To children who invent whole worlds in a vacant lot;
To the gang of '63: Paulette Groark, Kevin Gallardo,
and Raymond and Mark Long. —D.D.

In memory of Grandma Arlene, who grew up in an
old farmhouse, and was all parts Kindly Lady. —E.W.

Text copyright © 2017 by Denise Doyen.
Illustrations copyright © 2017 by Eliza Wheeler.

Library of Congress Cataloging-in-Publication Data available.

ISBN 978-1-4521-4589-1

Manufactured in China.

MIX
Paper from
responsible sources
FSC™ C008047
www.fsc.org

Design by Kristine Brogno.
Typeset in Museo Slab.
The illustrations in this book were
rendered in India ink with dip pens and
watercolors.

10 9 8 7 6 5 4 3 2 1

Chronicle Books LLC
680 Second Street
San Francisco, California 94107

Chronicle Books—we see things
differently. Become part of our
community at www.chroniclekids.com.

The POMEGRANATE WITCH

Written by **Denise Doyen**

Illustrated by **Eliza Wheeler**

chronicle books · san francisco

Beyond the edge of town,

where streetlights stopped and sidewalks ended,

A small boy spied a farmhouse in a field long untended—

And before its sagging porch, amid a weedy foxtail sea,

Found the scary, legendary, haunted pomegranate tree.

The gnarled tree loomed high and wide; its branches scraped the ground.

Beneath there was a fort, of sorts, with leafed walls all around.

Its unpruned limbs were jungle-like, dirt ripplesnaked with roots,

But glorious were the big, red, round, ripe pomegranate fruits.

The children whispered secret plans and spoke of desperate measures,
Delicious dreams of snatching, eating pomegranate treasures.
But rarely did they dare because there was a nasty hitch:
The tree was owned and guarded by the Pomegranate Witch!

The Pomegranate,
Pomegranate,
Pomegranate Witch.

No one could see her clearly, 'mid the dark and shadowed nooks.
Still, lore and pinkies swore the dreadful rumors of her looks;
Gossip painted her hands green, with twiggy fingers made to scratch!
And hearsay said her blood-red eyes stared through the thicker-thatch.

When new kids, disbelievers, crept up close to listen, look,

They'd hear witchcackle, "Hee, hee, hee," as branches shivershook.

And when her raven screamed, "Hey-*yaw!*" those kids would run in fear,

But not before the Witch's broom had bristle-spanked a rear!

And yet, the brave kept wandering back; the tree was like a thirst.

Forbidden fruit is tempting—pomegranates are the worst.

First one, then three, then five courageous souls rose to the test,

And thus, each autumn's Pomegranate Gang began their quest.

Some clever gangster-pranksters dug a foxhole in the field.

When they peered below the leaves? Witchy work boots were revealed!

Next, they scavenged broken racquets, rusty rakes, a dead tree limb;

What better tools to yank a pomegranate from its stem?

The Witch watched on, a veteran of siege and kinderbattle;
She'd seen such cardboard lean-tos and she'd heard their racquets rattle.
She knew that soon the gung-ho gang could simply wait no more—
So, switcheroo, the Witch declared the Pomegranate War.

The Pomegranate,
Pomegranate,
Pomegranate War.

"Now hear this! Pomegranate Gang, I see you in your ditch!
High noon! Tomorrow!" double-dared the Pomegranate Witch.
Shocked and scared—caught by surprise—the gang froze, firmly rooted;
Then one, then three, then five stood tall—and all of them saluted.

The Pomegranate War was on!
  The troops made preparation;
They plotted how to storm a tree
  in fruit-assault formation.

At noon, the watchbird cawed,

    "Hey-*yaw!*" The players took their places:

The Witch, she hunkered down;

    the gang spread out at twenty paces.

"Charge!" The gang dashed forward in a speedy, greedy race.

The fastest—within reach—got blasted, *splash!* right in the face!

Water cannons! Rushing, gushing, from a dozen hoses

Wound throughout, the spouts swashed into eyes and shot up noses.

They couldn't see! They couldn't breathe! Retreat was wet and muddy.

Still coughing, someone spluttered, "G-g-grab your bike, your rake, your buddy!"

In caravan, the gang embarked
on Plan B, as agreed,
And pedaling down the potholed street,
the raiders picked up speed.

Then buckets of black walnuts spilled—the Witch low-pitched them out!

As hard as marbles, scattershot, they rolled and bounced about,

Then bowled right under—*bump-bump-bump!* The wheels could not be steered!

The riders jumped, their drivers stumped—bikes toppled, wagons veered.

They chucked their vanquished chariots, regrouped and reattacked.
The big kids held up trash-can shields, the small rode piggyback.
Worn sneakers shuffled through the nuts, tin armor took the spray,
High eager hands reached up to where the pomegranates swayed. . . .

The tree! Enchanted tree, it sprang to life
  with thrashing might!
The branches walloped,
  whacked and
  slapped;
  the leaves
  put up
  a fight.

The pomegranates danced away
from clasping, grasping fingers.
Bushwhacked, the pom-marauders fled.
But one small robber lingered. . . .

For while the Witch pulled on the strings
　　and played mad puppeteer,
A sneak thief tiptoed through the gate
　　and crept around the rear.
He grabbed a fruit and twisted,
　　jerked and tugged—a dozen tries—
Then *snap!* Off he skedaddled
　　with his pomegranate prize!

His pomegranate, pomegranate, **pomegranate prize!**

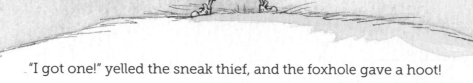

"I got one!" yelled the sneak thief, and the foxhole gave a hoot!

A rusty hammer cracked the husk; the gang split up their loot:

Six hundred sparkling seeds in papery slips kids ripped apart.

Hip-hip hooray! They'd won the day! The juice was sweet and tart.

A muffled laugh, the scuffle passed—things might have ended there,

For late that night, her harvest plucked the tree completely bare.

But neighborhoods have secrets, passed from year to ear to here:

There was one magic evening she was sure to disappear. . . .

On Halloween, the Witch flew off! She ventured far away,

To haunt with ghosts and jaunt with bats until the break of day.

And when she left? A kind insider hid away no more;

Each Hallows' Eve, the children knew who'd open up the door. . . .

The Kindly Lady, out she'd come! She'd sing and weed the path.
And no one blamed the shy soul for her sister's greed and wrath.
For when the Witch was home, she kept the farmhouse dark and scary.
But when the Kindly Lady reigned, the porch was lit and merry.

Her jack-o'-lanterns showed the way with jolly, square-toothed smiles.
She welcomed trick-or-treaters, "Have some cider. Stay awhile."
She showed them her pet peacock—lovely feathers, blue and green.
And then the kids and Lady toasted, "Happy Halloween!"

"Oh, dear," the Kindly Lady gasped,
and pointed toward the moon.
"I saw the Witch's shadow pass.
You'd best be off now, soon."

They swilled sweet dregs of cider; then the children grabbed their sacks.
She gave them each a feather—made them promise to come back.

And last, the Kindly Lady shared the best treat on the planet:
In every bag she dropped a big, red, round, ripe pomegranate!
"Goodnight!" she called. "I'll not see you 'til Halloween—next year."
They left her sweeping up; the sneak thief wiped a parting tear.

They skipped out past the haunted tree, its branches still and spent;
It slept the night the sisters switched—that's how the story went.
And not one child wondered who was who, or which was which,
The shy old Kindly Lady or the Pomegranate Witch.

The Pomegranate,
Pomegranate,
Pomegranate Witch.

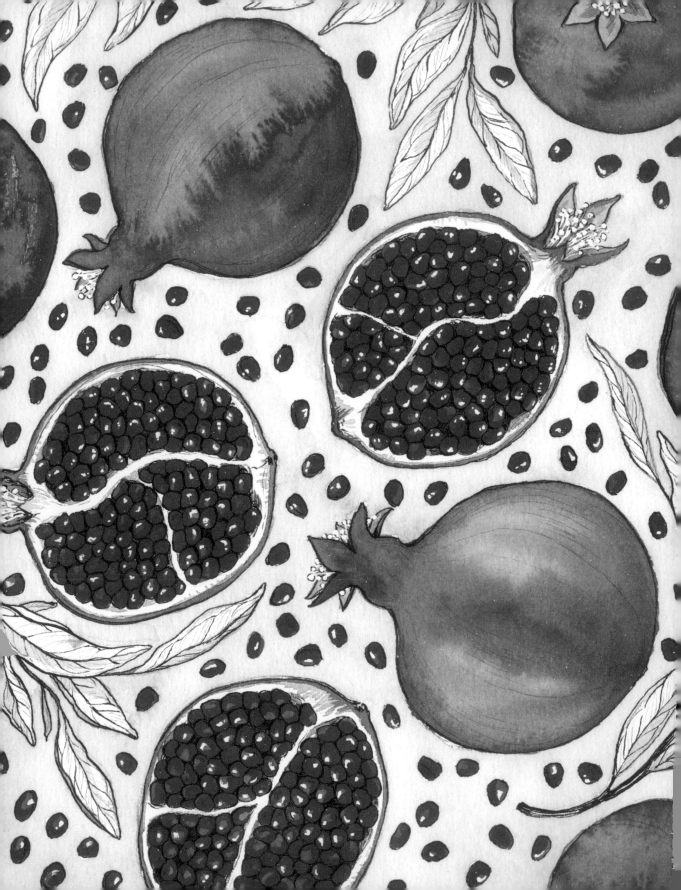